BRAVE MARGARET

An Irish Adventure

ROBERT D. SAN SOUCI

illustrated by SALLY WERN COMPORT

ALADDIN PAPERBACKS

NEW YORK LONDON TORONTO SYDNEY SINGAPORE

First Aladdin Paperbacks edition February 2002

Text copyright © 1999 by Robert D. San Souci

Illustrations copyright © 1999 by Sally Wern Comport

Aladdin Paperbacks

An imprint of Simon & Schuster

Children's Publishing Division

1230 Avenue of the Americas

New York, NY 10020

Also available in a Simon & Schuster Books for Young
Readers hardcover edition.

Designed by Lucille Chomowicz

The text for this book was set in Clearface Roman

The illustrations were rendered in pastels.

10 9 8 7 6 5 4 3 2 1

The Library of Congress has cataloged the hardcover edition as follows:

San Souci, Robert D.

Brave Margaret: an Irish Adventure / by Robert D. San Souci ;

Illustrated by Sally Wern Comport.—1st ed. p.   cm.

Summary: In this retelling of an Irish folktale, a brave young woman
battles a sea serpent and rescues her true love from a giant.

ISBN 0-689-81072-5 (hc.)

[1. Fairy tales 2. Folklore—Ireland.] I. Comport, Sally Wern, ill. II. Title.

Z7.S248Bt 1999 398.2'09417'02—dc21 98-16794

ISBN 978-0-689-84850-6

To DeDe Franquero
A Wonderful Friend & Outstanding Teacher

       —R. S. S.

 For Olivia
    —S. W. C.

ong ago a young woman named
Margaret lived alone on a
farm in County Donegal,
in the west of Ireland.
Between the wild sea banks and rugged crags
and cliffs, she found enough green grass to
raise a few cattle.

She was a red woman, with hair and
brows the color of burnished copper, skin
white as milk, and cheeks ruddy as fire glow.
She was wise as well as hardworking, and could
cast a spear or a herring net with equal skill.
She lived comfortably enough, but she longed
to learn what lay beyond the wide sea, or behind
the crags and cliffs.

One morning Margaret rose, washed her hands and face, said her prayers, ate her food, and went to lead the cattle from their byre. To her surprise, she saw a gallant ship, with lowered sails, anchored in the cove below her farm. Up the path climbed the handsomest man Margaret had ever seen.

"I am Simon, the son of the King of the East," he said. "My men and I are on a journey to the Kingdoms of the Cold, far to the north. But we have run short of supplies and must have meat to keep up our strength."

When Margaret heard him talk of places she had only dreamed of, she hungered to see more of the world. She had also fallen a bit in love with Simon. Nothing mattered but that she go to sea with him and his brave company.

"I will give you my cattle," she told him, "if you take me with you."

Simon refused at first, offering her gold beyond her cattle's worth. But she had made up her mind that he would have no cattle if he did not take her with him. At last Simon agreed that both Margaret and her kine would come aboard.

Then Simon turned the ship's prow seaward. His crew raised the red and white sails, and they overtook the wind ahead as easily as they outran the wind behind.

But soon the wind failed and a mist covered the sea. At Simon's command, his men lowered the sails and rowed for two days. Margaret put her back to an oar along with the others.

At dawn on the third day, the mist lifted. Then they found themselves adrift in strange seas. In the distance was a shore, low and gray. Overhead, the sky grew cloud heavy, fierce with thunder and lightning. Winds churned the waters to froth.

Suddenly a sea serpent erupted in a burst of spray. Simon shouted a warning to his men as the monster hurtled toward them. Towering over the ship, the creature roared, "Throw me the red woman, or I will swallow all of you!"

"Never!" cried Simon, drawing his sword. His men did the same. The monster hissed but hesitated.

Unnoticed, Margaret lowered a small boat and rowed away. "I will not be guilty of your deaths!" she cried. "What happens now is the will of God."

As soon as the serpent saw her, it turned from the ship, opened wide its jaws, and bore down on Margaret. The young woman stood, pulling an ax from the folds of her skirt. She knew she had but a single chance to defeat the onrushing beast. So she held herself in check until the monstrous jaws yawned wide in front of her. At the last moment she flung her ax deep into the creature's maw, wounding it terribly.

The dying monster thrashed about, raising huge waves. These swept Simon's ship far out to sea, and hurled Margaret's boat landward. She was tossed onto the shore, striking her head on the side of the boat, so that she was knocked senseless. Toward evening the falling rain woke her. She saw no trace of Simon's ship on the storm-wracked sea. Inland, Margaret spotted a light. This guided her to a rude stone hut. Through the single window she saw an old woman facing a peat fire.

She rapped on the door. When the old woman opened it, Margaret asked, "Will you give me shelter for the night?"

"I will," said the woman. "Come in."

She gave Margaret bread and milk, and a place to sleep by the fire. The cottage was unremarkable, save for two things: Upon the wall was a sword with a blade shining sun bright. Beneath it, a silver ring hung from a cord. When Margaret asked about these, the old woman replied, "I once lived in a castle at White Doon. A giant drove me from my home and took all except that ring and sword. Only the champion whose finger fits the ring can lift down the sword of light, slay the giant, and give me back my holdings.

"Many brave men have tried. But their fingers proved too big or small for the ring. They could not take the sword of light, so the giant slew them. The whiteness of White Doon is the whiteness of their bones."

The storm raged for days. Margaret stayed in the
cottage doing tasks the old woman set for her. Whenever
the wind and rain eased, she would scan the sea. But she
could find no sign of Simon. She imagined his ship dashed
to bits, and him clinging to some sea-bound rock.

"Storm or none," she vowed, "I will put to sea and
search for him."

But as Margaret prepared to leave, there was a knock on the cottage door. Opening it, she found herself face-to-face with Simon. For a moment they gaped in astonishment, then they hugged each other.

"I have been searching for you all this time," he said.

"And I was about to go in search of you," she said.

They gave no thought to the old woman watching them, until she told Margaret, "You'll not be going away just yet."

"Who's to say what I can and can't do?" Margaret snapped. Yet something in the woman's eyes chilled her.

Simon put his hand upon his sword hilt, but the old woman laughed. "You can no more draw your sword," she said, "than the woman can leave this place."

It was true. When Simon tried to draw his sword, his fingers grew numb, and his arm hung limply at his side. When Margaret tried to walk away, she found her feet frozen in place. They realized that the woman was a hag of sorceries.

"What is your price to free us?" asked Simon.

"The red woman stays until the giant at White Doon is slain," the hag answered. "Then I will give her to you and welcome."

"I will slay him, or die trying," vowed Simon.

When Margaret begged him not to go, he said, "You cannot keep me from this any more than I could keep you from sailing with me." Then he added tenderly, "And I know now that I cannot live apart from you."

The old woman said, "Try the ring on your finger. If it fits, you can carry my sword of light against the giant."

Simon untied the ring, but the circle of silver was too small for his finger. When he tried to take down the sword of light, he could not budge it from the wall.

"Away with you," the hag said, tying the ring back to the cord. "You are not the champion I await. But the woman stays; she will be the prize that draws a true champion."

"I will face the giant with my own sword," Simon declared.

Again Margaret begged him not to go, but Simon did not listen.

"One of the horses from my stable will carry you to White Doon," said the hag.

Helplessly, Margaret watched Simon ride toward the hills.

After a time the old woman stoked the hearth fire and tossed some herbs into it. In the flames Margaret saw White Doon, littered with the bones of fallen warriors. Over the field brooded a castle of black stone.

As Margaret gazed, Simon's horse galloped into view. At that moment the doors of the castle burst open, and the giant lumbered forth, his club raised. He bellowed:

Fee, fum, fo, fay,

What foolish mortal comes this way?

Churl or champion, king's son or knave,

One blow of my club puts you in your grave!

"For Margaret!" Simon shouted, charging with drawn sword. Bravely he fought, and several times he wounded the giant.

In the cottage Margaret prayed that Simon would deliver a fatal stroke. But in the end the giant swung his club, and Simon sprawled lifeless in the dust.

Shouting in shock and rage, Margaret spun about, frantic to strike back at the monster. On impulse, she snapped the ring from its cord. It slipped easily onto her finger.

"*I* am the champion you have waited for!" Margaret cried to the astonished old woman. "What fools we are for thinking it must be a man who slays that great, dirty giant!"

Margaret took down the sword of light.

Hurrying to the stable, she saddled a horse that
galloped swift as the March wind to White Doon.

When the giant heard her horse's hooves, he bellowed:

Fee, fum, fo, fay,
What foolish mortal comes this way?
Churl or champion, king's son or knave,
One blow of my club puts you in your grave!

Seeing Margaret, he threw back his head and laughed. But Margaret, spurred on by the sight of Simon's lifeless body, charged forward. Her sword of light bit deep into the giant's thigh, and his laughter ended in a bellow of pain. He swung his club, but Margaret wheeled her horse, ducking his blow. As their battle raged, Margaret's sword blows shattered trees. The stones of the black castle danced when the giant slammed the ground with his club.

At last Margaret cut the
monster's ankles, dropping
him to his knees. "For Simon!"
Margaret cried, and struck the
giant's head from his shoulders.

Dismounting, she knelt beside Simon's body, weeping bitter tears. Suddenly, the hag of sorceries appeared before her.

"Away with you!" cried Margaret. "You have cost me my dearest love!"

"Follow me," said the other. "What is done may still be undone."

Heartbroken yet hopeful, Margaret followed the old woman into the castle of black stone. There the woman lifted a green bottle from an oaken chest. "This is the water of healing," she said, uncorking it. She dabbed a drop upon her forehead. Instantly she became a youthful, raven-haired beauty.

Then the woman sprinkled the water of healing upon Simon, who immediately returned to life. After this, she gave Margaret and Simon purses filled with gold and silver, and bade them return to the shore where Simon's ship was anchored.

The crew hoisted sail. When they reached the
Kingdom of the East, the ruler, Simon's father, gave Margaret
a hundred thousand welcomes. Then came the priest of the
patens and the clerk of the bells to marry the pair. Their
wedding lasted nine nights and nine days, but their happiness
lasted a lifetime.

Author's Note

Adapted from the tale "Simon and Margaret" in

West Irish Folk-Tales and Romances,

collected and translated from the Gaelic by

William Larminie, published in 1893 by

The Camden Library. Additional details have come

from other stories in the collection,

and a variety of outside sources,

including The Land of Ireland *by Brian de Breffny,*

photographs by George Mott,

published by Abradale Press/Harry N. Abrams, Inc.